Sleeping Beauty

Including The Six Swans & The Princess and The Pea

igloobooks

Sleeping Beauty

here once were a King and Queen who seemed to have
everything anyone could wish for. They lived in a beautiful
palace and ruled over a happy country where all their subjects
loved them dearly. But there was one thing that made the King and
Queen very sad indeed: they had no children.

One morning, as the King was looking over some documents with his
courtiers, the Queen suddenly burst in.
"My dear," she said breathlessly, "I have great news!"
"And what might that be, my love?" asked the King.
"I'm going to have a baby!" exclaimed the Queen, excitedly.
The King was so delighted he dropped his map, burst into tears and gave
his wife a great big hug.

A few months later, the Queen gave birth to a little girl. And she was the
prettiest baby anyone had ever seen. She had big blue eyes, lovely blonde
hair and a perfect smile. The King was so taken with his child, he ordered
a national holiday on the day she was born. He and the Queen adored
their new daughter and spent many hours gazing lovingly at her.

"She's as beautiful as you, my dear," said the King fondly to the Queen.
"I'm sure she'll grow up to be as wise as you," the Queen replied.
"Thank you, my love. How blessed we are," said the King.

The King decided to hold a huge christening party for the new Princess, and invited people from far and wide. When the day came, everyone in the palace was excited. The cooks had been up all night preparing delicious food and the gardeners had been working for weeks to make the palace grounds look perfect.

The King and Queen also invited six fairies to the christening party, whom they hoped would bestow special gifts on the new Princess. One by one, they approached her crib.

"I bestow beauty on you," said the first fairy, gazing fondly down at the gurgling Princess.

"Joy," said the second.

"Wisdom," said the third.

"To be generous," said the fourth.

"Health," said the fifth.

But before the sixth fairy could bestow her gifts, the doors of the great chamber were suddenly flung open. There stood an old, ugly fairy that no one really liked, and were secretly a little afraid of.

"Why wasn't I invited to your party?" the old fairy asked, glaring at the King. "Well … I … umm, I'm not quite sure," stuttered the King, looking down at his shoes, feeling embarrassed. Everyone fell silent.

"I have a gift I'd like to bestow on the dear child."
said the old fairy, walking up to the crib and looking down at the Princess.

"My gift to you," she began, "is that when you reach the age of sixteen, you will prick yourself on the spindle of a spinning wheel and you will die!" And with that, she turned around and walked angrily out of the palace. The poor Queen burst into tears. Then a lovely, clear voice rang out. It was the sixth fairy.

"I haven't bestowed my gift yet," she said. "I cannot undo the terrible curse of the old fairy but I can change it a little. My gift to you, little one, is that you won't die if you prick your finger on a spindle but, instead, you will sleep for one hundred years." From that day on, the King banned all use of spinning wheels. If people wanted any wool to be spun, they had to send it to another land.

Time passed, and everyone started to forget the old fairy and her curse. The Princess grew up to be beautiful, healthy, wise and generous.
Everyone in the country loved her.

On her sixteenth birthday, the King gave a grand party. For a present, he had a beautiful dress made for her. It was the first proper grown up dress the Princess had ever worn. It was a lovely, green silk dress, with an elegant, high collar, and it was so long it reached the floor.

The Princess invited all her friends to the party. After eating a huge birthday lunch, they decided to play hide-and-seek.
"You won't catch me," said the Princess, running quickly away.
Trying to find a place where nobody would find her, she climbed a stone staircase to the very top of one of the palace's towers.

At the top was a small room where an old lady sat at her spinning wheel. She had been there for years. "How nice to see you, my dear," said the old lady with a warm smile.

"What beautiful thread you're making!" exclaimed the Princess. "May I try the spinning wheel?"

She sat down at the wheel and began to spin but, as soon as she did so, the spindle pricked her finger. With a small cry, she fell to the ground and fell fast asleep. At that very moment, everybody else in the palace, and in the palace grounds, fell asleep too.

Many years went by and, little by little, a huge thorn hedge grew around the palace. It was so thick that the few people who tried to fight their way through gave up. In time, the palace, and the people sleeping in it, were completely forgotten.

Then, one day, a Prince from a far off land rode by and saw one of the palace's gleaming towers in the distance. In a nearby village, he asked if anybody knew to whom it belonged. But nobody did. It was too long ago. Then, a very old man said his grandfather had told him that, many years ago, a palace had stood there, but no one had been able to cut through the thorn hedge to get to it.

This story made the Prince curious, and he decided to try to cut through the dense hedge. He took out his sword, and started to hack his way through the thorns. Without warning, the thorn bush suddenly fell back, and cleared a path for him right up to the palace itself.

To his great surprise, the Prince saw people draped all around the grounds. They all seemed to be sleeping. The Prince warily made his way into the Palace. It was exactly the same inside: people everywhere, and they were all fast asleep! Treading carefully, the Prince slowly made his way up the grand staircase, passing sleeping people as he went.

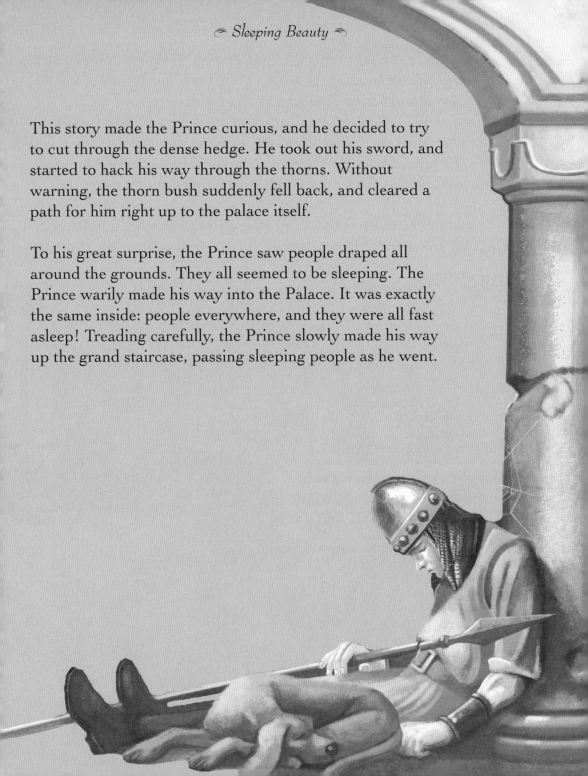

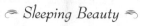

At the top of the stairs was a large oak door. He pushed it open and couldn't believe his eyes. In front of him lay a lovely Princess who was also sound asleep. She was so beautiful, he gasped out loud. In one swift movement, the Prince knelt by her side and kissed her gently on the lips. To his utter astonishment, her eyes slowly opened, and she began to wake. The Prince looked into her deep blue eyes and realized she was the girl he had been waiting for all his life.

At that moment, everyone else in the palace woke up, too. It was exactly one hundred years since the old fairy had cast her evil curse.

The Prince and Princess decided to marry.
The palace was cleaned of its cobwebs and
their wedding took place soon after. It was a
joyous day for everyone and the Prince and
Princess lived happily ever after.

The Six Swans

In a land far, far away, there once lived a King with his six sons and a daughter. His children wanted for nothing in life. They studied with the best teachers, ate the finest food and wore only the most magnificent clothes. But, one day, the King married again. Unfortunately, the new Queen was an angry, bitter woman who hated her step-children on first sight. She decided to get rid of them all. First, she sent the young Princess away to live in the country and, not long after, cast an evil spell on the young Princes that turned them into six perfect, white swans.

"Go," she told them. "Fly far from here and find somewhere else to live."

When she was sixteen, the Princess was brought back to live in the palace. When the Queen saw how beautiful the Princess had become, the Queen became so jealous she smeared the poor girl's skin with walnut juice, tore her dress and made her hair look wild and tangled.

"Look at this peasant girl," cried the Queen, dragging the Princess by the hair to the King. "See how disgusting she looks. How can she be a King's daughter?"

The confused King agreed with his wife that the filthy girl standing in front of him could not possibly be his daughter, and ordered her to leave the palace at once.

The Princess walked into the nearby woods where she found a stream to bathe herself and wash away the foul walnut juice. She felt so lonely and sad, she began to cry. She longed to see her brothers again but had no idea where to find them.

As the sun began to set, and the lightness of the day turned into the darkness of the night, she looked up and saw six swans flying towards her. They flew lower and lower until they landed close to where the Princess stood. Then something strange happened. The swans began to change shape, shedding their feathers and turning into human form. With a gasp of astonishment, the Princess realized that the six swans had turned into her six long lost brothers.

The Princes told their sister that ever since they had been turned into wild swans, they had lived in a far off land across the sea. They came back to their homeland only once a year to fly over the palace where they were born. They also told her that, although they were swans in daylight, as soon as night fell, they turned back into human form again. "At dawn we will change into swans, and fly back to the land where we live. Will you come with us?" they asked their sister.

"I will," the Princess replied. "You are my brothers whom I love dearly. I never want to be parted from you again."

That evening, the Princes worked hard, building a net of vine and willow bark that would carry the Princess. At first light, they turned back into swans and soared into the sky, bearing the weight of their sister between them. They flew for many hours without rest. The only thing the Princess saw was the glittering sea, below. But, as the day drew to its end and there were no signs of land, she began to worry. "It will soon be dark," she thought. "If we don't find land soon, my brothers will turn back into human form, and we will all fall into the sea and drown."

Shortly after, to her immense relief, the Princess saw land in the distance. Leaving the sea behind them, the swans set her down gently in a leafy forest glade. They turned back into the Princes again as soon as their feet touched the ground.

"Welcome to your new home," they said happily. That night the Princess had a dream. She dreamed that a wise old woman told her that her brothers could be freed and remain human if she were to collect a special nettle that grew in the forest. She had to weave the nettles into six magic cloaks which should be put around her brother's shoulders. Once this was done, the evil spell would be broken. But the old woman warned the Princess she must not speak until the cloaks were finished. If she uttered just one word, the cloaks would not work their magic. Early the next morning, convinced that the dream was an omen, the Princess started to gather the special nettles.

Later that day, the King of the land was out hunting, and noticed the Princess picking her nettles. He thought she was the most beautiful girl he had ever seen.
"Who are you?" he asked.

But, remembering the old lady's words, the Princess remained silent. The King was so enraptured by this beautiful, mute girl he decided to take her back to his palace with him and make her his Queen.

The whole country celebrated on the day of the marriage. Everyone, that is, except the King's Archbishop, who believed that the Princess was really a witch of the forest who had tricked the King into marrying her. "Of course she's a witch," the Archbishop thought to himself. "That's why she won't speak to anyone."

After she was married, the Princess continued her work on the magic cloaks in secret. One day, she ran out of the special nettles. That night she stole out of the palace and made her way to the forest, where she began to collect more. Unbeknown to her, the suspicious Archbishop had followed her. He rushed back to the King and told him what he had seen.
"I knew it all along!" cried the Archbishop. "The girl is collecting nettles to use in magic potions. She is a witch! She must be burned at the stake!"
When faced with this charge the Princess, as ever, did not speak a word. The poor King loved his wife dearly but, in the face of the Archbishop's evidence, had little choice. With a heavy heart, he ordered that she must undergo a witch's punishment and be burned at the stake.

The Princess was dragged to the cells and, one week later, was taken by cart to the place of execution. As the cart made its way through the cobbled streets, the Princess worked furiously on the last of the special cloaks. As she neared the dreaded stake, there was a murmur from the crowd as six beautiful swans flew down and sat on the unlit bonfire. "This is an omen," some of the people whispered. "This surely means that our Queen is innocent!"

As the executioner reached for her hand to lead her up to the stake, the Princess quickly gathered up her nettle cloaks, jumped from the cart and threw them over the six swans. At once, the swans changed into the six handsome Princes. At last, they were free from the curse! They would never change into swans again.

"Now that my brothers are free, I can speak, my love," said the Princess to the King. When she told him the story of their stepmother's curse, the kindly King wept with pity for them.

"I nearly made a dreadful mistake," he said. "You and your brothers have shown much courage. I hope you will lead happier lives from now on. The Princes will always have my protection while they live in this land."

The brothers built palaces for themselves near to the royal palace. They visited their sister often and lived happily for the rest of their lives.

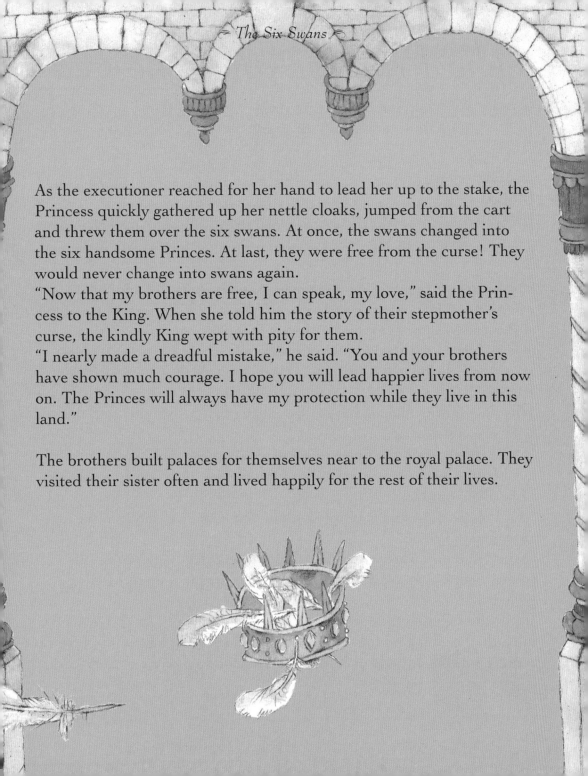

The Princess and The Pea

In a distant land, there lived a Prince who decided one day, that he wanted nothing more in the world than to marry a beautiful Princess. His parents, the King and Queen, agreed that he was now old enough to marry and wished him well in his hunt.

For the next two years he journeyed far and wide to find his perfect wife. But the Prince was a very choosy person and, although he met lots of Princesses along the way, he always found something wrong with them. They were either too short or too tall. Too fat or too thin. Too happy or too sad, or just too nice!

When he returned home, he was very upset that he couldn't find the right Princess to marry.

"There, there," said the Queen, comforting her son. "I know it must be terribly upsetting for you, dear, but I'm sure that the right Princess will come along one day."

"But I might be an old man by the time that happens," moaned the unfortunate Prince.

"Now," said his father, the King, "things aren't that bad. You're still young, rich, handsome and a Prince! You're bound to find the right girl soon."

"But, when?" cried the Prince.

In truth, the King and Queen were a bit fed up with their son (who was acting a bit spoiled) and decided to send him away to one of their other castles for a complete rest.

One night, there was a terrible storm. Thunder and lightening filled
the sky. The windows rattled and the wind whistled around the rooms
of the old castle. As the storm raged on, there was a knock on the huge
castle door. The Queen opened it and standing before her was a young
girl who was shivering from the cold and the rain.

"My goodness," said the Queen. "What a dreadful night to be outside.
You're soaked through, my dear. You'd better come in and we'll find you
some dry clothes."
"How kind of you," said the girl.

The Queen led her to the drawing room where she could dry herself by
the large, crackling fire.
"Do you live nearby?" asked the Queen.
"No, Your Majesty," replied the girl. "I'm a Princess from another land.
My carriage is stuck in the mud, a little way down the road."

As the Queen and the girl talked, the Queen began to realize that this young Princess might make the perfect wife for her son. She wasn't too short or too tall. She wasn't too fat or too thin. She wasn't too happy or too sad and, although she seemed very nice, she didn't seem to be too nice. But the Queen wanted to make sure the girl was a real Princess so that they wouldn't be disappointed. She had an idea how she could find out.

"My dear," said the Queen. "We can't possibly let you leave on such a terrible night as this. I insist that you stay here tonight. I will get the maids to make up a bed in one of the guest bed-chambers."

"That's very kind of you, Your Majesty," said the girl, who gave a little curtsy, and went off to have a steaming hot bath.

The Queen told her maids to collect as many mattresses and quilts as they could find and to stack them on the guest's bed. Then, she went to the castle kitchen where she picked out a single, dried pea from a jar. She gave the pea to one of the maids, and ordered that it be placed underneath the bottom mattress.